At **THE DAVID BECKHAM ACADEMY** every day is a footballing adventure. Boys and girls come along to learn about the sport, develop their skills and have fun. But it's not just about tricks and flicks . . . As David Beckham knows, the real secret behind being a Premier League player is understanding the importance of dedication, teamwork, passion and having belief in yourself. In these pages you can meet football-mad children and follow them as they live out their dreams at The Academy.

SO STEP INSIDE AND JOIN THE FUN!

Want to know what some of our readers thought of this book?

'I liked Oliver, and the best bit of the
story was when Luke and Louis
become friends again'
Jude, age 7

'I really liked the food fight'
Ryan, age 7

'I wouldn't change anything
about this story!'
Hattie, age 9

'My best bit was the food fight'
Jordan, age 10

'This story is great – I give it
10 out of 10!'
Jake, age 8

'My favourite part of the story was when
the English and the French teams had an
argument and became competitive'
Stephen, age 10

'I liked the bit when the French team
and the English team get together and
play the Pittsburgh Titans'
Joe, age 9

EGMONT

We bring stories to life

First published in Great Britain 2009
by Egmont UK Limited
239 Kensington High Street, London W8 6SA

Text and illustrations © 2009 Beckham Brand Ltd
adidas, Predator, the 3-Bars and the 3-Stripes are registered
trademarks of the adidas Group, used with permission

Text by Jason Loborik
Cover and inside illustrations by Adam Relf
Cover photography by Anthony Mandler
Design by Becky Chilcott

ISBN 978 1 4052 4525 8

5 7 9 10 8 6 4

A CIP catalogue record for this title is available
from the British Library

Typeset by Avon DataSet Ltd, Bidford on Avon, Warwickshire
Printed and bound in Great Britain by the CPI Group

THE DAVID BECKHAM ACADEMY

LE FOOTBALL

EGMONT

CONTENTS

NEW ARRIVALS

Luke Chapman was having the best game of his whole life. He'd just scored two brilliant goals for his team and no one was going to stop him making it a hat-trick.

'Go on, Luke, you can do it!' yelled his lanky friend Max, who was playing in goal on Luke's side.

'This is my chance!' Luke muttered as a striker on the other team dribbled the ball towards him. With amazing speed, Luke flew at it, sliding in for a perfect tackle. The ball sprang free and Luke was up and after it in a flash. He got it under control with ease, dodged past a defender, then went charging towards the goal.

'Go on!' cried Oliver, another friend, as Luke's foot connected hard with the ball. It slammed straight into the back of the net.

'Yesss!' roared Luke, as the whistle blew for full time.

'We did it!' cheered Max. He started singing a victory chant: 'Three–nil, three–nil, three–nil, three–nil, *three–nil*!'

Luke was grinning as the three boys headed back to the changing rooms. It was only his second day at The David Beckham Academy, but in that time he'd made two new mates and was playing better football than ever before.

'You were awesome,' said Oliver, slapping Luke on the back.

'Cheers,' said Luke. 'Guess I had some luck in that game.'

'*Luck?*' repeated Oliver. 'More like pure skill, I reckon. I wish I was half as good as you!'

'You're pretty good yourself, Olly,' smiled Luke.

'Well, maybe, but I bet you're the one who'll be a professional in a few years.'

'Yeah, well . . .' he shrugged.

Embarrassed, Luke ran his hand through his short brown hair. He was used to being the best player on the pitch, but he didn't like to go round boasting about it.

'Anyway, you made some world-class tackles just now,' said Luke. 'And you're brilliant at tactics.'

'Oh, tactics is just classroom stuff,' said Oliver, pulling a face. 'It's what you do on the pitch that counts.'

'Having short fat legs doesn't help much, does it?' said Max behind them, playfully trying to trip Oliver up.

'Hey, stop it,' snapped Oliver. 'I didn't notice you doing much just now!'

'What do you mean?' said Max, surprised.

'Well, every time a striker came anywhere near you, Luke rushed him and got the ball away!'

'Maybe he did,' frowned Max. 'But it takes real skill to be a goalie, y'know!'

'What, you mean standing up straight and trying not to fall asleep?' Oliver teased.

'No, *I don't* mean that,' replied Max.

'Oh, you mean being tall and lanky?' giggled Oliver. 'Cos that's not skill either.'

'Oi, you! I made some good saves in that game!' Max protested.

Luke laughed at his two friends. They just couldn't resist winding each other up!

● ● ●

Later on in the changing room, the boys had just finished getting dressed when they suddenly heard a loud voice booming across the room.

'OK, everyone, could I have your attention, please? I've got a very important announcement to make!'

The voice belonged to Frank Evans, head coach of The Academy. He had grey hair, a big grey moustache and right now his eyebrows were knitted together crossly. Everyone stopped talking and listened.

'Wonder what it is?' whispered Oliver. 'Is David Beckham coming or something?'

'*Ssshhh!*' hissed Max.

Mr Evans looked sternly at Max and Oliver, then cleared his throat importantly.

'Now, as you all know, the next World Cup is just a few months away, and to celebrate we've been taking part in a special football exchange scheme. For the rest of the week a boys' team from France will be joining you. This only happens once in a while, so I hope you'll all give them a very warm welcome.'

Just then, Max put his hand up and started waving it about.

'Yes, Max, what is it?' said Frank.

'Do you want us to thrash them?'

Everyone sniggered and Frank cleared his throat again.

'I expect you to do your very best, of course,' he said. 'But the most important thing is that you show them everything that's good about English football. I want to see teamwork, dedication and good, all-round sportsmanship.'

Whispers of excitement echoed around the room and Oliver turned to Luke, grinning. 'Let's show them what's good about English footy,' he said. 'You'll blow them away!'

One by one, the French team filed into the changing room, looking slightly nervous.

'Right,' continued Frank. 'I'd like you all to line up and give our guests a welcoming handshake.'

As the two lines of boys shuffled past each other, they all smiled and shook hands.

'Hi, I'm Luke,' said Luke as he came to the last boy in the line.

'Louis,' replied the boy. He was taller than Luke, with long dark hair. He looked very strong.

'It's really good here,' said Luke. 'You're going to have a brilliant time.'

He held out his hand and Louis shook it in silence, then turned away sharply and walked off with his teammates.

Luke was left slightly puzzled. 'Hmmm,' he murmured to himself. 'Was it something I said?'

DRIBBLE TROUBLE

The next hour was skills training on the pitch and everyone in Luke's team was jumping around excitedly.

'OK, England, are you ready for this?' yelled Chris the coach.

Luke smiled. All of the children at The David Beckham Academy were normally split into teams named after great footballing countries. In honour of the arrival of the French team, however, the kids had been grouped into just two teams – England and France. To Luke, it almost felt like he was representing his country for the first time.

'I hope you've all drunk some water,' continued Chris. 'Cos you're going to be sweating buckets, I can tell you!'

The children laughed. Just then, Luke caught sight of Louis and his friends walking towards them. A couple of them were yawning.

'Look,' said Luke, quietly. 'It's that new guy.'

'You mean Louis?' said Max. 'Yeah, he seems pretty cool. He told me he's France's team captain.'

'Really?' asked Luke. 'He wouldn't even talk to me earlier.'

'He's probably just tired,' chirped Oliver. 'One of them told me their team bus was stuck in traffic for hours.'

As the French boys approached them,

one of them turned to Max.

'*Ça va?*' asked the boy, whose name was Philippe.

'Er, right, er . . .' began Max. '*Oui, oui. Je suis Max.*'

Philippe frowned and Oliver screwed up his face at Max's reply.

'He just asked how you are,' Oliver said, 'not what your name is!'

'Did he?' said Max. 'Trust you to know that, swot!'

'It is OK,' said Philippe, laughing. 'I can speak English very well.'

Louis turned to Luke with a serious look on his face, as if something was on his mind.

'I was watching your team this morning,' Louis said. 'I think you could have scored more goals.'

'Oh, you reckon?' said Luke, frowning. 'We did win three–nil, you know . . .'

'Yes, yes, I saw that,' continued Louis. 'But I saw the other team's defence. They were *terrible*! Why did you spend so much time defending instead of attacking?'

'So what if we did?' said Luke, getting annoyed. When it came to football he couldn't stand being criticised.

'I am sorry, I don't mean to upset you,' said Louis. 'It is just that the French never play like that.'

'So how do *you* play then?'

'Well, we always try to attack and take every chance to score.'

'But there's more to football than that.'

'I do not think so,' replied Louis.

'Yes, there is!' said Luke, raising his voice. 'Everyone knows you need a good defence to win a match . . .'

'OK, OK,' said Louis, holding up his hands. 'I only say what I think.'

Before Luke could say anything else, Chris the coach started giving the children instructions.

'Right. Now our visitors have joined us, I want you all to practise dribbling with the ball,' he said, pointing at two long lines of cones on the pitch. 'The first person in each line dribbles in and out of the markers. When you reach the end, turn round and carry on all the way back, then pass the ball to the next person. Any questions?'

Max put his hand up.

'Is it a competition, Chris?' he asked hopefully.

'Not today, Max,' answered Chris. 'I just want you to learn to control the ball properly first.'

'Oh, right,' said Max.

'Remember not to hit any of the cones,' said Chris. 'Right, off you go!'

Minutes later, the boys had organised themselves into two rows and Max and Philippe were the first off. Dribbling really wasn't Max's best skill and Louis was shouting out tips on what to do.

'You are kicking too hard,' he called, as the ball went spinning off in all directions.

'I'm doing my best!' said Max.

By the time he'd reached the end of the cones, Philippe had already turned round and was almost back at the start.

'See?' said Louis. 'Look how Philippe does it. He can dribble twice as fast as you!'

'Yeah, and you can talk twice as much as anyone as well,' grumbled Luke under his breath. As his turn came up, he realised he was going to be dribbling alongside Louis.

'OK, ready for this?' smiled Luke.

'*Oui!*' replied Louis.

'Remember, it's not a competition,' said Chris sternly, as the two of them sped off.

It was soon obvious that Louis was the

better dribbler though, and he weaved in and out of the cones like an expert. Luke focused hard, determined to keep up.

'They're definitely having a race, aren't they?' said Max, watching the pair keenly.

'Yep, looks like it,' nodded Oliver.

As Luke rounded the last cone, his heart sank. Somehow Louis had speeded up and was getting further ahead.

'Come on, Luke, try to catch me!' called Louis, as he neared the finish line.

'No thanks,' replied Luke hotly. 'I'll just take my time.' But as he crossed the finish line, Luke was secretly cross with himself for coming second.

'As I said, it wasn't a race,' Chris reminded him, noticing how fed up he looked.

Luke glanced up at Louis, who was laughing with all his teammates, an annoying grin on his face.

It was *a race, and I blew it*, Luke thought to himself. *But next time I'll show Louis who's best!*

PITCH BATTLE

'That Louis is so full of himself,' grumbled Luke as he warmed up for the afternoon match. Over lunch, Team England had been told they would be playing a friendly against Team France.

'Philippe reckons he's pretty cool when you get to know him,' said Oliver helpfully. 'He says Louis is always putting his foot in it. He speaks first, then thinks about it afterwards!'

'Hmmm,' snorted Luke. 'Well, maybe he shouldn't bother speaking at all.'

'Oh, come on,' Oliver laughed. 'Give him a chance!'

'Yeah, but did you hear him at lunchtime?' said Luke.

'No, what did he say?'

'He kept going on about how they were going to beat us ten–nil.'

'Well, we'd better prove them wrong,' shrugged Oliver.

'Yeah, you're right,' laughed Luke. 'We'll give them a right thrashing and teach Louis a lesson!'

Just then, Louis called across from where Team France was warming up.

'Hey, Luke,' he shouted. 'I hope your team is prepared. We want a decent game today!'

'No probs,' Luke shouted back. 'Just wait till we get on the pitch!'

'And do not play so defensively,' continued Louis. 'Attack more for a change.'

'Well, why don't you try using some skill for a change,' Luke retorted. 'Instead of kicking the ball up the field and hoping for the best!'

'Come on, Luke,' said Oliver calmly. 'Just ignore him.'

'I can't help it,' said Luke. 'He winds me up, that's all!'

Just then, Chris came running on to the pitch, ready to start the game. The air was tense as the whistle blew for kick-off. In no time at all, Louis was charging into the English half, dribbling easily past their midfielders.

'Tackle him!' shouted Luke, as Louis broke through England's defence.

A defender rushed forwards, but Louis just changed direction swiftly, cutting back inside before thundering on towards the goal, leaving the helpless defender stranded.

'Come on! Get him!' yelled Luke at his defence, but it was too late. With amazing power, Louis' foot struck the ball straight into the net.

'*Ooooouuuuuuuiiii!*' screamed Louis, punching the air triumphantly.

Luke was gutted. They were one–nil down in the first minute! What if the French ended up giving *them* a complete thrashing instead?

'Come on!' he yelled at his team. 'We're going to show them that England's the best!'

The players all nodded at Luke, and

drifted towards the French half, passing the ball between themselves.

'What are you doing, Luke?' shouted Oliver from the subs bench. 'You'll leave us exposed to a counter-attack!'

But Luke wasn't listening. He was on the ball and sprinting towards the French goalmouth. Two defenders came at him and he kicked the ball wildly, desperate to score. The goalie caught it easily.

'To me! To me!' yelled Louis in French. The goalie quickly lobbed the ball up-field and Louis started running with it.

'Oh, no!' whimpered Max as he saw Louis come storming towards his goal, with hardly a defender in sight. Once again, Louis slammed the ball into the net.

'I don't *believe* this,' groaned Oliver. 'Luke keeps pushing everyone forwards and

forgetting about our defence!' In fact, Oliver hardly dared watch any more as, time and again, the French attackers tore through the weak English defence.

In the second half, they got another easy break. Dodging a lone defender, Philippe crossed to Louis who then neatly flicked it into the corner of the goal!

'This is terrible!' gasped Oliver. 'You've

got to get back in defence, Luke!' he called. 'We're leaking goals like a sieve!'

Luke didn't reply – he hated being bossed around on the football field.

'That is three–nil,' called Louis as he trotted past Luke.

'Yes, I know,' sulked Luke.

'I do not want to give you advice, but if I were you I would get your team to –'

'Look, mate, just keep it to yourself, all right?' cut in Luke, getting angry. 'You're not one of the coaches!'

'OK, I was only trying to help,' snorted Louis, running back to his own half. Luke was more determined than ever to try and win.

'I've *got* to do something or we're going to get thrashed,' he muttered.

As play carried on, he finally managed

to win the ball from the skilful French players. He surged forward into the opposition half, fighting off tackle after tackle. Finally getting a clear run at the goal, he fired the ball past the keeper and into the net.

'*Yessssssss!*' yelled Oliver, jumping up and down in excitement.

A few minutes later, Luke got another

break. Inside the French penalty box, he passed to an attacker who watched Luke continue his run, before passing it back. Luke took the ball in his stride and slotted it home past the helpless goalkeeper.

'Goooal! That's three–two!' he yelled, punching the air. He looked up at the clock, and his face fell again. 'Oh, no – only two minutes till full-time!'

Despite Luke's two goals, the French weren't about to give up their lead. Yet again, Louis and Philippe ran easily into the badly defended English half. They flicked the ball to each other over a couple of defenders' heads, setting up the perfect strike for Louis, who blasted another one home.

'That's it,' said Luke, feeling sick. 'We've had it.'

As the final whistle blew, he just couldn't bear to look at anyone, especially Louis. He ran off the pitch and into the building, heading for the Hall of Fame.

'At least I'll get a bit of peace here,' he said to himself, as he walked past the display of David Beckham's football memorabilia.

Out of breath, he slowed down and noticed all the shirts that had belonged to famous international players. He stopped to look at David Beckham's framed jersey.

'I bet you never had to put up with a silly show-off like Louis!' he said with a sigh.

CLASSROOM CLASH

Next morning, Luke and his friends were late for their tactics lesson, and they all bustled noisily into the classroom.

'Sorry, Chris,' said Luke, panting. 'My alarm didn't go off.'

'Glad you could make it, gentlemen,' said Chris sternly. 'Now find a seat, please, quick as you can.'

'There is one here . . .' said Louis as Luke walked by his table.

'I'm not sitting anywhere near you,' muttered Luke, and he took a spare seat at the front, alongside Oliver and Max.

'OK, let's make a start,' said Chris brightly, flicking the switch on the overhead projector. An image of a football pitch appeared on the screen with lots of red dots marked on it. 'Can anyone tell me what this is?'

Oliver's hand shot up. He loved the classroom stuff – it was the only place

where he felt on a level with everyone else.

'Yes, Oliver?' said Chris.

'It's the standard four-four-two formation, Chris,' said Oliver. 'Four in defence, four in midfield and two in attack . . .'

'. . . don't forget the goalie,' added Max.

'Good,' said Chris with a smile. He pointed at one of the positions near the goal. 'Now, can anyone answer me this? Your full-back has possession of the ball. What should they do with it?'

This time, Louis put his hand up.

'That is simple,' he said. 'The defender should make a long pass to the star striker on his team. The striker will then dribble around everyone in the other team's half and score.'

Louis folded his arms as if that were the end of the matter, but Luke threw his hand up, obviously desperate to speak.

'All right, Luke, out with it before you burst!' chuckled Chris.

'That's not right, Chris,' said Luke. 'The defender should pass the ball to the other defenders to pull the opposing team out of position. You need to keep possession then gradually move forwards –'

'But what is the point of doing that?' cut in Louis.

'It's obvious,' replied Luke, not looking around. 'Against a good team, a striker will never be able to do it all himself. You need to create space.

'That is *so* typical of dull English football,' said Louis, shaking his head.

'No, it isn't,' replied Luke, whirling

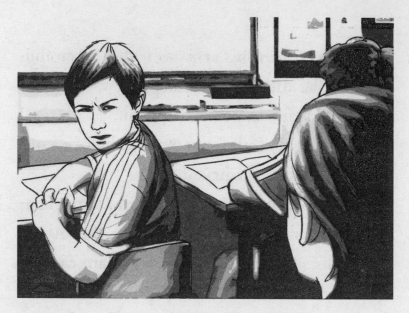

round in his seat. 'It's the proper way to play.'

'But it is so boring to watch,' said Louis.

'No, it *isn't!*'

'Yes, it is!'

'Now settle down, you two,' warned Chris. 'It's good to talk about this stuff, but let's have bit of respect for each other's point of view. OK?'

'Sorry, Chris,' said the boys, although they both still looked unhappy.

'Let's try another question, shall we?' said the coach quickly.

'Right, the goalie's just made a save,' said Chris, pointing towards the goal. 'You can see various dots for the defenders who are close to him. How should he get the ball back into play?'

Luke's hand was in the air even before Chris had finished speaking.

'He should look for a defender to throw the ball to,' he said. 'That means that his team can keep possession rather than kick it away.'

'*Non, non, non!*' insisted Louis. 'Why do the English think only about defence all the time? That is not how you score goals. The goalkeeper should kick the ball up the field to the star striker, and then he will dribble past the other team and score. Simple!'

Chris let out a long sigh and flashed up more diagrams. But every time he asked a question, he got the same answers.

'Build up from the defence!' said Luke.

'Pass to the striker!' argued Louis.

'That's quite enough,' said Chris. 'I'd just like to point out to you two that French and English footballers play together all the time in the Premiership. How do you reckon they manage it?'

Oliver nodded slowly, thinking he had the right answer, but Luke suddenly piped up again.

'Obviously, the French players must learn the right way once they've played with the English,' he said.

'It is the other way round, I think!' called Louis from the back of the class.

'Right, I've really had enough of this!' scolded Chris. 'Luke and Louis – I don't want to hear any more from you two until you can show some proper respect for each other. Understand?'

The two boys nodded sheepishly and sat in silence, arms folded, while the rest of the lesson carried on. Neither would ever dream of backing down. After all, this was football they were talking about. The most important game on the planet!

FOOD FIGHT

The next day, Luke did his best to keep out of Louis' way during training. In fact, by lunchtime he'd almost forgotten about him and was just looking forward to eating.

'I wonder what's on today?' said Max as three of them filed into the canteen. 'I'm starving!'

'Same here,' agreed Luke, his stomach rumbling loudly.

Just as he went to take a tray, he heard a voice behind him.

'Hey, Luke, so sorry you lost the argument yesterday.' Luke turned round and saw Louis grinning at him.

'I didn't lose it,' growled Luke. '*You* did.'

'But why can you not see there is a much better way to play football than the way you play?' said Louis.

'Cos there isn't one,' replied Luke.

'Oh, come on, Luke,' said Oliver, tugging at his arm. 'Let's just get something to eat!'

Luke allowed himself to be led away. He got his meal then went and sat down while Louis and his friends sat at the table in front. As they all began eating, they suddenly heard loud voices coming from the kitchen.

'You don't know what you're talking

about,' said a gruff voice. 'I know how to cook spaghetti. Been doing it for years!'

'Who's that?' asked Max.

'Sounds like Chips, the head chef,' giggled Oliver.

'I tell you, you have cooked it for too long. It has gone mushy!' came an even louder voice, which sounded French.

Max laughed. 'The chefs must be doing this exchange thingy as well,' he said.

'And they're not the only ones who aren't getting on,' added Oliver, nodding at Luke.

'Our chef is right,' piped up Louis from the next table. 'I do not like the taste of this food!'

'OK,' said Luke behind him. 'Try eating this then!'

And, with that, he grabbed his fork –

which had a lump of half-eaten baked potato on the end – and flicked it at Louis. *SPLAT!* It hit him right in the back of the head.

'What . . . where did that come from?' said a startled Louis, pulling bits of potato out of his hair.

'Behind you!' snapped Luke. 'Now, put a sock in it – or else!'

'Or else what?' said Louis, turning round.

Luke went to pick some more food off his plate, but Louis was too quick for him. The boy picked up a half-eaten chicken leg and chucked it at Luke's table. It missed Luke but hit Max on the side of his head.

'Ouch!' he cried.

'Ha, ha! Rubbish shot!' shouted Luke.

'I was aiming for *his* head!' replied Louis.

Next, Luke scooped a big spoonful of baked beans up off his plate and flicked them at Louis and his friends.

'Urrrrrrgh!' winced Louis, turning to his friends. 'Right, get them!' he yelled in French.

The French boys sprang into action and started throwing handfuls of food at Luke, Max and Oliver, whooping with laughter.

'Quick, grab your trays!' shouted Oliver, and the three of them picked up their dinner trays to use as shields against the flying food missiles.

'It's working!' said Max, as chicken legs went pinging off in all directions.

'Haven't I always said you need a strong defence?' Luke laughed. He plucked

up the courage to peek over the top of his tray. 'OK, guys, maybe we should stop before we get into troub—'

SPLAT! A big slice of lasagne hit Luke right between the eyes. 'Oh, *yuck!*' he cried.

Just then, the two chefs came bursting out of the kitchen, wondering what all the noise was about. Chips opened his mouth to speak, but quickly found it full of baked potato as he went striding into the crossfire.

'Stop this *at once!*' bellowed a loud voice suddenly.

It was Frank Evans. He stood in the canteen doorway, his face bright red. Luke noticed some new boys close behind him, trying hard not to snigger. They were very tall and were wearing really flashy football kit.

'Did you two start this?' said Frank, glowering at Luke and Louis.

'Er . . . yes, Frank,' said Luke quietly.

'I've heard all about your silly disagreement, and it's got to stop,' continued Frank. 'Do you understand?'

'Yes, Frank,' said Luke and Louis together.

Louis turned to Luke and smiled mischievously through the bits of food that were sliding down his face. Luke couldn't help smiling back. Maybe Louis wasn't so bad after all.

'Now, before you clean up all this mess, I want to tell you the real reason I came in here,' Frank continued, turning to the boys in the doorway. 'I'd like you to meet the Pittsburgh Titans.'

Max put his hand up.

'Are they on the exchange as well?' he asked.

'Yes, they're from America,' explained Frank, 'and goodness knows you should all be ashamed of the impression you've made!'

'Will any of them be on our team?' frowned Oliver.

'No,' said Frank, 'you'll be playing *against* them. I want you to put together the best team you can from all the English and French players!'

Luke and Louis gaped at each other in horror as Frank walked out of the door, the Pittsburgh Titans following close behind.

'Well, if we have to play together, you had better learn the French way quick,' said Louis.

'No *way*,' snapped back Luke. 'I'm not doing that. I'd rather not play at all!'

TEAM EFFORT

Early the next day, Luke, Max and Oliver were warming up as usual with the rest of Team England, standing away from their French visitors. Max was busy admiring Luke's spotless kit.

'Wow,' he said. 'Where are all those food stains from yesterday?'

'We got my kit cleaned at our hotel,' replied Luke, glumly. 'Cost a fortune. My mum's taken it out of my pocket money.'

Just then, Chris came running on to the pitch.

'Right,' he said cheerfully. 'Everyone remember what Frank said yesterday?'

'Yes,' the boys chorused.

'Good,' smiled Chris. 'Let's see how quickly you can make a European team. Remember, there's got to be an equal number of French and English players.'

'But how can we do that when there's eleven on a team?' frowned Oliver.

'Well, with five players on the subs bench, that's sixteen altogether,' replied Chris. 'Eight English players, and eight French ones. Off you go!'

In their two separate huddles, the boys started chattering away, trying to work out who should play, and in which position. Chris watched them for a while and then called for quiet.

'I was expecting you all to talk

together,' he said, 'not completely ignore the other group!'

'Sorry, Chris,' said Luke, 'but we don't think this is going to work.'

'Why not?' asked Chris.

'Cos the English way of playing is the best. If we have French players on the team, they'll just mess everything up and try to play their way!'

'And then we'd lose,' added Max.

'That is not true!' said Louis from the French group. 'You do not stand a chance without us. The only way we will win this game is if *every* player is French!'

'Huh, like *that's* going to happen,' tutted Luke.

But ten minutes later, with Chris overseeing them, the boys had somehow managed to agree on a brand-new team. Luke was picked as the best defender, and Louis was up front as the star striker. As usual, Max was in goal and poor Oliver was back on the subs bench. Louis still wasn't happy though.

'*Non*, *non*, *non*, Chris,' he argued.

'*Now* what's the matter?' asked Chris.

'We need to play the best football in this game, yes?'

'Yes.'

'Well, the best football in Europe is played *in France*. That means we should have an all-French team!'

'That's *so* lame!' cut in Luke. 'Everyone knows that England is the home of football. We should definitely have an all-English team to play against them.'

'What, and lose the game?'

'No, we wouldn't!'

As the boys started arguing once again, Oliver tried to make himself heard.

'Er, I reckon we could play pretty well together,' he said, slowly. 'Luke can organise the defenders and Louis can score goals up front. Easy, really!'

But neither boy even heard him, they were so busy squabbling. Chris had finally had enough.

'Right, that's it, I'm not listening to any more of this,' he insisted. 'I really can't believe how much energy you've wasted with all these rows, and now you've dragged your own teams into your silly arguments as well! Just get on that pitch and play like proper sportsmen!'

Louis and Luke trudged on to the field with the rest of Team Europe. Max spotted the Pittsburgh Titans at the other end, doing their warm-ups.

'Luke, look over there,' he pointed.

Luke turned and saw the Titans in their trendy red-and-blue strip, doing all sorts of fancy stretches in time with one another.

'They look pretty good, don't they?' said Max, chewing his lip.

'Yeah, guess so,' agreed Luke.

'We can still beat them though,' said Oliver hopefully.

By now everyone was watching the Americans as they started flexing their muscles. They suddenly looked rather big – and scarily strong.

'Erm . . . I take that back,' whispered Oliver. 'I reckon we're done for!'

Their warm-ups finished, the Titans got into a huddle and started chanting at the tops of their voices:

Pittsburgh Titans have come to town,
Going up the league, and you're going down!
Mess with us and feel the heat,
Pittsburgh Titans can't be beat!

They ended the chant with a huge roar, then leaped in the air, giving each other high fives.

'Uh-oh,' said Luke to his friends. 'This is going to be a disaster. If only we had a half-decent team to play with!'

Oliver kept watching the Americans nervously as he walked to the subs bench, then he glanced back at Luke and Louis.

'I don't believe it,' he gasped to himself. 'They're completely ignoring each other.'

Sure enough, Luke and Louis had walked off in opposite directions without speaking. Jaideep, one of the other subs, shook his head.

'You'd think they'd talk about tactics or something,' he said. 'Even if it was just for a second!'

'Not those two,' said Oliver, glumly. 'It looks like we've lost before the match has even started. If we don't find some way of playing together, we're completely sunk!'

THE BIG GAME

'Please, please, don't let this be a complete disaster!' said Oliver to no one in particular, as the big match finally kicked off.

From the start, Louis managed to grab possession and zoomed forwards with the ball.

'Pass it back, Louis!' yelled Luke from his position in defence. 'You're going to lose it!'

Sure enough, the Americans closed in on Louis. He saw off some fierce tackles, but very soon the Titans had won the ball and were running towards Europe's end of the pitch, Louis and Phillippe hot on their heels.

'What are they doing?' Max shouted to Luke. 'Why won't they stay forward and let the defence and midfield tackle them?'

'They obviously don't trust our defence,' Luke shouted back as he prepared to tackle the approaching Titans.

Philippe went flying towards the ball, but the Titan strikers were faster. Dodging Philippe's tackle, one of them pressed on towards Team Europe's penalty box.

'Rob! Danny! Get in there!' yelled Luke to the nearest defenders, but it was already too late. With all the members of Team Europe getting in each others' way, the ball whizzed through the air and struck the back of the net.

'Why do you not sort out the defence?' said Louis, running past Luke. 'Now we're a goal down in the first minute!'

Luke was furious, but he was ready next time the Titans tried to break through. He launched himself at a striker and got the ball away. He passed it back to Rob, and the defenders carried on passing between themselves, looking for a chance to get it up the field.

'Come on!' bawled Louis. 'Pass it to me!'

'No chance,' replied Luke, and he started running with the ball himself. Two Titans bore down on him and the only player he could see to pass to was Philippe.

'You're not getting it either,' muttered Luke.

'Just pass it!' yelled Philippe, but the

Titans had already snatched the ball away from Luke. They thundered back towards the goal, planting another one in the net.

'Why did you not pass?' shouted Louis. 'We could have easily scored.'

'Yeah, well, you never pass it to us, do you?' snapped Luke hotly.

'This is even worse than I thought,' sighed Oliver on the bench as, yet again, Luke refused to pass up the field. Dodging an American tackle, he chipped it back to Rob who was surrounded by Titans in the penalty box. Rob bravely tried to head it away, but the American in front was quicker – and taller. He beat Rob to the ball and guided it expertly into the top of the net.

'No, no, *no!*' said Oliver, stamping

his feet in frustration. When he next dared to look up, he saw the Titans had pushed deep into the European half yet again. Suddenly, their striker slipped, losing control of the ball. Louis and Luke both sprinted towards it.

'It is mine,' barked Louis.

'No, it's mine!' yelled Luke.

'Get back in defence!'

'No way. Get back up front!'

And with that, the two boys slammed into each other, banging their heads.

Hardly believing his luck, the Titans' striker was back on his feet and after the loose ball again, heading for the goal.

'Block it!' shrieked Oliver, but it was too late. The ball struck home bringing the score up to a crushing four–nil.

The whistle blew for half-time and, as

usual, Louis and Luke were busy blaming each other.

'Why did you not let me get it?' snapped Louis. 'I shouted first.'

'I was nearest,' spat Luke, rounding on him. 'And I was just trying to defend, like defenders are *supposed* to!'

From the subs bench, Oliver could hear every word and decided he couldn't put up with this stupid nonsense any more.

'WILL YOU TWO JUST SHUT UP!' he yelled as loudly as he could.

Everyone just stopped and stared at him. No one had ever heard Oliver shout like that before.

'Right,' said Oliver shakily, not quite believing what he'd just done. 'Do either of you remember the tactics we learned the other day?'

Luke and Louis just stared at him blankly.

'Oh, come on, you must know what you've got to do!'

The two boys looked at each other sheepishly but neither wanted to be the first to speak.

'All right, I'll tell you,' sighed Oliver. 'The English players need to man the defence. They need to tackle the opposition and feed the ball up to the French players in attack. Simple.'

Louis was about to speak, but Luke didn't want to listen to any more. He ran off into the building, making up an excuse about needing the toilet. Instead he made his way to the Hall of Fame. He needed time alone to think.

Once again, he looked at the famous players' names on all the shirts. A thought struck him. David Beckham had played with stars from loads of different countries. There were Brazilian shirts, Spanish shirts – even a French shirt hanging up there.

'Maybe Olly's right,' he said to himself. 'If Beckham can play with footballers from all round the world, why can't I?'

He thought about Louis. The boy really got on his nerves, but he suddenly realised how similar they both were. Each thought his way of playing football was the best and that the other was completely wrong. No wonder they were losing the game. He sighed deeply.

'If we're going to win this, one of us needs to do something,' he decided.

Feeling a bit better, he ran back on to the pitch and jogged up to Louis.

'Now then, Louis,' he said, giving the French boy a big slap on the back. 'You and I are going to win this game!'

'Er . . . but how?' asked Louis in surprise.

'By working together,' replied Luke. 'It's the only way.'

Louis thought for a second, then slowly nodded.

'*Oui*, you are right,' he said at last. 'But we are four—nil down. How are we going to do it?'

JOINING FORCES

The whistle blew for the second half, and both teams burst into action. Oliver had joined Team Europe in midfield, replacing a boy who'd given his all in the first half. He bounded around, full of energy, glad to be off the subs bench for once.

As usual, the Titans were quick to gain control, and their striker went storming down the wing, looking for a gap in the European's defence.

'Oh no you don't,' breathed Luke, dashing towards the attacker. He slid in to make a superb tackle and got the ball away. Looking up, he spotted Louis in the distance.

'It's yours!' yelled Luke as his foot struck the ball hard, sending it sailing into the air. It passed over a couple of American defenders and into Louis' path.

'Oh, cool pass!' shouted Max in goal.

Meanwhile, Louis had avoided being tackled by passing across to Oliver, who neatly bounced the ball back to him a bit further forwards. Louis picked it up again, dodged round a defender, then gave the ball an almighty *THWACK*, sending it straight into the back of the net!

'*Goooooooal!*' roared Louis and Oliver, high-fiving each other.

'*Yesss!*' screamed Luke. 'We can do this!'

And, sure enough, the game suddenly

began to look very different for Team Europe. Luke stayed back to man the defence. Every time the Titans came on the attack, Luke and the English defenders tackled hard, gained control, then passed up the field to the strikers.

With both the French and English playing together at last, their confidence began to return and they soon began to find the net.

'This is unbelievable,' Oliver shouted at Luke, as Louis made a superb volley, driving home another goal. 'That's four–all!'

Luke was worried though. With Max about to take a goal kick, he looked up at the clock and saw there was just one minute left. They may have equalised to earn themselves a draw, but that wasn't good enough. They had to win!

'Push up,' he yelled at his teammates.

Max passed the ball to Luke, who sprinted forwards, his heart pounding. The whole arena seemed to go deathly quiet as he went to kick the ball. What if he messed it up, sent it completely wide? The whistle was about to blow. Almost all of Team Europe was surging into the penalty area, looking to connect with the cross as it came. It would need to be inch-perfect.

Grabbing the moment, Luke swung his foot down sharply and connected hard with the ball, launching it into the air. As it flew towards the far end of the field, he held his breath, hardly daring to look.

At the other end of the pitch, Louis saw the ball heading towards the edge of the Titans' penalty area. He sprang forwards and cushioned it on his chest.

The referee brought the whistle up to his mouth. Only seconds left . . .

With perfect timing, Louis sprang backwards, his foot coming up to the ball in a dramatic overhead kick. The ball flew towards the goal, with the Titans scrambling to block it. The goalie made a dive, desperate to make the save, but it missed his outstretched fingers by a whisker and went spinning into the goal! The whistle blew with an ear-shattering *PEEEEEEEEP!*

Team Europe roared with delight as they jumped around in the penalty area, cheering for all they were worth.

'We did it!' gasped Oliver in delight. 'Isn't that *incredible*!'

Luke came running up to join the celebrations, and Louis allowed himself a

smile. He ran forwards to Luke and met him with a big high five.

'Not bad,' he said to Luke, pausing. 'For an English player, of course!'

Luke laughed.

'We did it,' he beamed. 'I never thought it would work, but we made a brilliant team in the end.'

'Yes, we did,' replied Louis, breaking out into a smile at last. 'And I suppose we could not have done it without each other!'

Just then, Chris came up and patted Luke on his back.

'You did really well there, Luke,' he said. 'I'm proud of you. You put your personal arguments behind you for the good of the team. Just like a true sportsman!'

Luke smiled happily, watching Max and Oliver still jumping around for joy. This just had to be the best feeling in the whole world!

'In fact,' continued Chris, walking off the pitch with the two boys, 'as you guys played together so well, I reckon you should take your team to the LA Academy for a rematch with the Titans.'

Louis and Luke gaped at each other in surprise.

'What, *really*?' asked Luke.

'What time is the plane leaving?' laughed Louis.

The two of them headed off, chattering excitedly about how they would be even better next time. Suddenly, a thought struck Luke and he stopped in his tracks.

'Hey, Louis,' he said. 'Any chance we could swap shirts?'

'*Oui* – but why?' replied Louis, puzzled.

'Well, have you seen that display of football shirts inside?' asked Luke. Louis nodded. 'Well, when I get home I'm going to have my own version in my bedroom – my very own Hall of Fame!

TURN THE PAGE TO READ A SNEAK PREVIEW OF

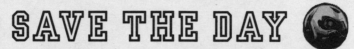

SAVE THE DAY

THE THIRD BOOK IN THE DAVID BECKHAM ACADEMY SERIES!

SEARCH AND RESCUE

'This is ridiculous!' moaned Charlie as he tipped the laundry basket over his bed. 'Where *are* they?' He rummaged through dirty socks and T-shirts, chucking aside anything that didn't have blue stripes and five fingers – which was everything.

'My gloves have got to be here *somewhere*!' he continued as he tossed the basket to one side and dropped to the floor, wriggling on his stomach to explore the darkness beneath his bed. Unfortunately, all he found were a couple of football stickers from last season's collector's album, and the mouldy remains of an apple core.

Sliding out from under the bed, he tossed the apple core into the wastebasket then, after a second's thought, emptied the bin on to the floor and began to search through its contents.

'Have you seen my goalkeeping gloves anywhere, Bob?' he asked the only other occupant of the room. 'I can't go to The David Beckham Academy without them!'

Bob sat in silence and watched as Charlie dragged the duvet and pillows off his bed, pushing a hand between the sheet and the mattress to feel around. But then Charlie hadn't really expected a reply in the first place – Bob *was* the family's pet cat.

'You're useless!' Charlie sighed as Bob curled up on the crumpled duvet and closed his eyes, but he crouched to scratch his pet behind the ears anyway. He scanned his bedroom as the cat purred softly.

The walls were covered with posters of football players and clippings of special matches cut from newspapers. In pride of place on the wardrobe door was a picture of his hero, David Beckham.

Charlie had been excited when his parents announced that they had booked him on a three-day course at The David Beckham Academy. He'd read in *Football Crazy* magazine that The Academy was putting together a special team, and he desperately wanted to wear the goalkeeper's shirt – and his lucky gloves, of course.

Charlie stared at the smiling face of

David Beckham on the wardrobe. At the bottom of the poster was one of his hero's favourite sayings: 'Believe In Yourself'.

That's no help, Charlie thought. *How can I believe in myself if I can't find my — ah, the wardrobe!* He leaped to his feet suddenly. He hadn't looked on top of the wardrobe for his gloves. Dragging his bedside table across his room, Charlie pushed his alarm clock and copy of *Football Crazy* magazine on to the floor. There'd be plenty of time to tidy up when he returned as the official goalkeeper of The Academy's new team. Jumping on to the table, he stretched up to search the top of the wardrobe.

Charlie had always been small for his age, but that didn't matter when there were handy items of furniture around to give you a boost. He felt around the pile of board games and old toys – and that's when he heard the scream.

It wasn't the kind of scream you get when someone's watching a scary movie, or when your sister finds a spider in the bath. It was more like the scream you'd hear when your mum walked into your bedroom and discovered that you'd completely trashed it in less than twenty minutes flat. Still, it was enough to make Charlie lose his balance and fall. He toppled backwards, his arms wind-milling wildly. Luckily, the thick duvet cushioned his fall – and Bob didn't even wake up.

'I didn't hear the explosion!' said Mum as Charlie scrambled to his feet and pulled the duvet back over his bed.

'What explosion?' asked Charlie.

'The bomb,' replied Mum. 'A bomb has gone off in here, hasn't it?'

'Sorry!' said Charlie. 'I just can't find my lucky gloves, and I'll never get into The Academy team without them.'

'Just as well you made me pack them in your bag last night then, wasn't it?' smiled Mum, straightening the duvet.

Charlie's cheeks flushed red as he remembered. 'I think I'm just nervous!'

'Not just nervous,' said Mum. 'You're late as well. Go and get in the car!'

As Mum followed Charlie down the stairs, Bob opened one eye and checked that he was finally alone. He yawned and settled back down to sleep. Peace at last!

On the way to The Academy, Charlie told his mum all about the special team the coaches were putting together. He told her how all the players would be picked from the kids training there over the coming weeks. By the time Charlie's mum dropped her son off at the entrance to The Academy, she was ready for a nap herself. Charlie rushed inside, already pulling on his goalie gloves as he prepared for the best three days of his life.

Since he was a little late, Charlie was handed his kit and asked to change quickly before being shown straight through to the pitch where the rest of his team was already gathered. He arrived just as the team's coach, Woody, was assigning positions to the group of eager young players in front of him. He paused as Charlie's tiny frame appeared at his waist.

'You must be Charlie,' said the coach.

'We still need a defender and someone to play on the left wing. Which position would you prefer?'

'Neither, I'm in goal!' grinned Charlie as he waved his gloved hands in front of his face.

Collect all the books in
The David Beckham Academy range

STORYBOOKS

Twin Trouble	ISBN 978 1 4052 4524 1	£4.99
Le Football	ISBN 978 1 4052 4525 8	£4.99
Save the Day	ISBN 978 1 4052 4526 5	£4.99
Bossy Boots	ISBN 978 1 4052 4527 2	£4.99

ACTIVITY BOOKS

How-to Handbook	ISBN 978 1 4052 4669 9	£4.99
Ultimate Football Sticker Book	ISBN 978 1 4052 4670 5	£4.99

ANNUAL

2010 Annual	ISBN 978 1 4052 4644 6	£7.99

EGMONT PRESS: ETHICAL PUBLISHING

Egmont Press is about turning writers into successful authors and children into passionate readers – producing books that enrich and entertain. As a responsible children's publisher, we go even further, considering the world in which our consumers are growing up.

Safety First
Naturally, all of our books meet legal safety requirements. But we go further than this; every book with play value is tested to the highest standards – if it fails, it's back to the drawing-board.

Made Fairly
We are working to ensure that the workers involved in our supply chain – the people that make our books – are treated with fairness and respect.

Responsible Forestry
We are committed to ensuring all our papers come from environmentally and socially responsible forest sources.

**For more information, please visit our website at
www.egmont.co.uk/ethical**

Mixed Sources
Product group from well-managed forests and other controlled sources
www.fsc.org Cert no. TT-COC-002332
© 1996 Forest Stewardship Council

Egmont is passionate about helping to preserve the world's remaining ancient forests. We only use paper from legal and sustainable forest sources, so we know where every single tree comes from that goes into every paper that makes up every book.

This book is made from paper certified by the Forestry Stewardship Council (FSC), an organisation dedicated to promoting responsible management of forest resources. For more information on the FSC, please visit **www.fsc.org**. To learn more about Egmont's sustainable paper policy, please visit **www.egmont.co.uk/ethical**.